Keep the music
in your heart!

~Bobcat
Bob

ISBN 978-1-933212-79-1

Published by Commonwealth Editions, an imprint of Applewood Books, Inc.,
Box 27, Carlisle, Massachusetts 01741

Visit us on the web at www.commonwealtheditions.com
Visit Shankman and O'Neill on the web at www.shankmanoneill.com.

A portion of the proceeds from the sale of this book will be donated to the
New Orleans Musicians Assistance Foundation.

Printed in China.

10 9 8 7 6 5 4

ce the cavemen hummed,
maids sang, and the natives drummed,
been music in the air,
could find it everywhere.

Bands were roaming near and far,
From Mexico to Zanzibar,
From Iceland to the Ivory Coast
And all the places you like most.

There were bands in Greece and France
And anywhere that folks could dance.
Just find a map and pick a spot—
There was no place that bands were not!

d though the bands were very good,
every land and neighborhood,
he very best would make their way
New Orleans, in the U.S.A.

The Bourbon Street Band is Back

BY ED SHANKMAN
ILLUSTRATED BY DAVE O'NEILL

Commonwealth Editions
Carlisle, Massachusetts

That is where the great bands met.
And one was even better yet.
It was the grandest of the grand—
Bobcat Bob and his Bourbon Street Band.

The Bobcat wore a cool French hat.
He wore it forward, straight and flat.
When someone wears a hat like that
You know that must be one cool cat.

(He had hat-itude. And cat-itude!)

While Bobcat Bob attacked the drums,
A snapping turtle snapped his thumbs.
Warblers warbled. Catbirds mewed.
Kingbirds led and the cowbirds mooed.

On the horns were three raccoons,
A crawfish and a pair of loons.
On several of the lighter tunes,
A frog sat in to play the spoons.

To help old Bobcat keep the pace,
A gator played the stand up bass.
Those players really rocked the place,
As sweat poured down that gator's face.

Those who heard them say they played
Like lightning mixed with lemonade.
And that, I think you will agree,
Is just as good as a song can be!

When players play like that, you know
Word's bound to spread about the show.
Soon people came from miles around
To hear them make their special sound.

The band played fast and it played loud.
The louder it played, the bigger the crowd.
A song might start out sweet and mild.
Then came the drums and the crowd went wild!

I wish you'd seen them on the stage,
Back then when they were all the rage.
They played like wind. They played like fire.
They raised the roof, and raised it higher.

They played all night and weren't done
'Til morning came and they raised the sun.
They raised it up with a sound so bright
It washed away the dark of night.

Not every band can raise the sun
But one that can is lots of fun.
So people cheered with sheer delight,
And somehow all the world seemed right.

That is until a certain show,
One certain night, not long ago,
When halfway through a happy song,
It seemed that something went quite wrong.

The music stopped. There was no sound.
The people gasped and looked around.
Somehow, it seemed, a change had come
That stopped the bass and hushed the drum.

It hushed the loons and three raccoons.
It hushed the frog who played the spoons.
And all the others on the stage
Were silent as an empty page.

Then Bobcat Bob took off his hat
And left the stage in seconds flat.
And just like that, without a choice,
The great New Orleans lost its voice.

And with the music, went the sun.
Without the band, it came undone.
It slid back down below the ground,
And darkness rose up all around.

The whole world watched as silence came.
And all agreed it was a shame.
What was the cause? Who was to blame?
Would New Orleans ever be the same?

For months, the sun stayed out of sight.
And through those months of endless night,
Through all the time that darkness stayed,
No songs were heard. No notes were played.

Of course, without a music show,
The people had no place to go.
They stayed at home and locked the door,
And wished that things were like before.

Now life is strange, and things can change.
Sometimes they simply rearrange.
Some go from good to bad, it's true.
But they can change for the better too!

And that is what occurred the day
That music found a way to play.

It started
with a
single beat.

TAP

They heard it out
on Bourbon Street.

Then another. TAP

Then a third. TAP

And then they say a fourth was heard. TAP

Out in the dark, these beats were beated. Some just once, and some repeated.

It was a drum! There was no doubt! A drum was calling people out!

A drum was saying, "Come out here.
Ignore the dark. And have no fear."
The people heard it loud and clear,
And soon began to gather near.

TapTap
Tippity
Tap

TapTap
Tippity
Tap

TapTap
Tippity
Tap

TapTap
Tippity
Tap

And who do you suppose they found
Pounding out that drumming sound?
Was that a cat in a cool French hat?
It was Bobcat Bob they were looking at!

And as the drum picked up the pace,
The gator joined with his stand up bass.
Soon the horns began to blare,
And then sweet voices filled the air.

And somewhere just behind the loons,
There seemed to be the sound of spoons.
These players clearly had the knack.
Bob and his Bourbon Street Band were back!

In fact, the band seemed even more
Exciting than it was before.
The notes were sweet and strong and clear.
They shook the heart. They kissed the ear.

They rose, those notes, like flames and sparks.
They floated through the streets and parks.
They reached so high, and went so far,
You could have heard them on a star.

And what was that off to the right?
What thing could be so big and bright?
It lit the sky, it warmed the air.
What was that giant thing up there?

"The sun," they cried. And it was true.
At last the sun was shining through.
A brilliant ray that brought the day
And made the darkness run away.

Now other bands were playing too,
And bigger crowds came into view,

As thousands danced and sang along,
In a great parade of sun and song.

Now bands took turns and people cheered.
They cheered each time a band appeared.
They clapped for every song they knew.
And then for every new one too.

It's good to cheer with all your might.
And those folks clapped a lot that night.
But the biggest hand in all the land
Went to ...

Bobcat Bob and his
Bourbon Street Band.